ttle Tiger book belongs to:

_____

_____

_____

*For Michael, with all my love – C F*

*For Emily – S M*

LITTLE TIGER PRESS
An imprint of Magi Publications
1 The Coda Centre, 189 Munster Road, London SW6 6AW
www.littletigerpress.com

First published in Great Britain 2009
This edition published 2010

Text copyright © Claire Freedman 2009
Illustrations copyright © Simon Mendez 2009
Claire Freedman and Simon Mendez have asserted their rights
to be identified as the author and illustrator of this work under
the Copyright, Designs and Patents Act, 1988

A CIP catalogue record for this book is available
from the British Library

Printed in Singapore
LTP/1500/0045/0610

2 4 6 8 10 9 7 5 3

# One Winter's Night

Claire Freedman          illustrated by Simon Mendez

LITTLE TIGER PRESS
London

It was deepest, darkest winter. Wild snow
blizzards had howled through the woods
for days and the animals had been hiding
in their dens, cold and hungry.

But tonight, suddenly, all was quiet and
the sky was clear.

Fox peeped from his snowy den. Out of
the darkness appeared a lone figure,
a badger, gleaming silver in the moonlight.

"Hello," Badger called gently. "Please, I'm so hungry. Do you have any food to share?"

Fox frowned. He had hardly enough food for himself. But there was such a kind look in Badger's eyes. Fox felt he *had* to help him.

"Wait here," he said.

"Thank you," Badger smiled, gratefully
taking the few berries Fox offered.
Then off Badger went into the snow,
head bent against the bitter wind.

Mouse was much too cold and hungry to sleep.
As she tossed and turned in her bed, suddenly
she heard footsteps outside. "My, oh my!"
she gasped. "Who's out at this time of night?"

"Hello!" a silvery figure called softly.
"Please, I'm very hungry. Do you have
   any spare food?"
      "I've nothing at all!" Mouse grumbled.
"There's no food anywhere!"
      "I understand," Badger nodded,
   and he turned to go.

Mouse listened as the heavy crunch of
Badger's footsteps slowly faded. Badger had
seemed so gentle and caring. Yet she had
turned him away.

"Wait!" Mouse scampered after him.
"Hare lives nearby. Maybe she can help!"

Together, Mouse and Badger
struggled to Hare's house.
The wind whipped. Snowflakes
swirled. But somehow, even in
the shadowy dark, Mouse felt
safe beside Badger, his warm
eyes twinkling like bright stars.

Girls are **amazing.** So shout it out loud —

"I'm a GIRL!   I'm FANTASTIC!
I'm strong, brave and proud!"

MARIE CURIE

EMMANUELLE
CHARPENTIER

CLARA BARTON

ALEXA CANADY

Now, how many girls have **invented** a way
to make people's lives a bit better each day?

ELIZABETH BLACKWELL

ROSALIND FRANKLIN

FLORENCE NIGHTINGALE

HUALAN CHEN

They've **discovered** the causes of coughs, spots and sneezes
and learned how to treat many nasty diseases.

A girl can **explore**
a hot jungly place,

or float in a rocket ship
way out in space.

Girls can **fly planes** or **dive** under the sea.

Yes, girls can be **ANYTHING** they want to be.

A girl can find clues

to help **solve**

tricky crimes.

Or **speak out for others**
at difficult times.

When a girl is determined, she **always** succeeds.
Her **courage** and **strength** are what everyone needs.

THE NEWS

Girls are amazing.
So shout it out loud —
"I'm a GIRL! I'm FANTASTIC!

I'm strong, brave and proud!"

And the girl I love best in the whole world is YOU. Dream BIG, special girl. Tell me, what will YOU do?

## Claudia Gordon — Lawyer
First deaf African American female attorney in the US

## Maryam Mirzakhani — Mathematician
Winner of the Fields Medal, 2014

## Arunima Sinha — Mountaineer
First female amputee to climb Mount Everest

## Marin Alsop — Conductor
First female conductor at the *Last Night of the Proms*

## Serena Williams — Tennis Player
Tennis champion and icon

## Jane Goodall — Primatologist
Ethologist, anthropologist, and UN Messenger of Peace

## Nicola Adams — Boxer
First female and openly LGBTQ person to win a boxing gold at the Olympics

## Sue Wimpenny — Builder
Builder and CEO

## Sirimavo Bandaranaike — Politician
The world's first female prime minister

## Malala Yousafzai — Human Rights Activist
Youngest winner of the Nobel Peace Prize

## Karen Gaffney — Swimmer and advocate for people with disabilities
First person with Down Syndrome to complete a relay swim across the English Channel

## Peng Lei — Businesswoman
Co-founder and CEO of her own company

## Chimamanda Ngozi Adichie — Author
Winner of the MacArthur Genius grant

## Valentina Tereshkova — Cosmonaut
First woman in space

## Josephine Reynolds — Firefighter
First female British firefighter